In
1935 if you wanted to
read a good book, you needed
either a lot of money or a library card.
Cheap paperbacks were available, but their
poor production generally mirrored the quality
between the covers. One weekend that year,
Allen Lane, Managing Director of The Bodley Head,
having spent the weekend visiting Agatha Christie,
found himself on a platform at Exeter station trying to
find something to read for his journey back to London.
He was appalled by the quality of the material he had to
choose from. Everything that Allen Lane achieved from that
day until his death in 1970 was based on a passionate belief
in the existence of 'a vast reading public for *intelligent*
books at a low price'. The result of his momentous vision
was the birth not only of Penguin, but of the 'paperback
revolution'. Quality writing became available for the price of
a packet of cigarettes, literature became a mass medium
for the first time, a nation of book-borrowers became a
nation of book-buyers – and the very concept of book
publishing was changed for ever. Those founding
principles – of quality and value, with an overarching
belief in the fundamental importance of reading –
have guided everything the company has
done since 1935. Sir Allen Lane's
pioneering spirit is still very much alive
at Penguin in 2005. Here's to
the next 70 years!

MORE THAN A BUSINESS

'We decided it was time to end the almost customary half-hearted manner in which cheap editions were produced – as though the only people who could possibly want cheap editions must belong to a lower order of intelligence. We, however, believed in the existence in this country of a vast reading public for intelligent books at a low price, and staked everything on it'
Sir Allen Lane, 1902–1970

'The Penguin Books are splendid value for sixpence, so splendid that if other publishers had any sense they would combine against them and suppress them'
George Orwell

'More than a business … a national cultural asset'
Guardian

'When you look at the whole Penguin achievement you know that it constitutes, in action, one of the more democratic successes of our recent social history'
Richard Hoggart

Three Trips
The Short-Story Writer as Tourist

JOHN UPDIKE

PENGUIN BOOKS

PENGUIN BOOKS

Published by the Penguin Group
Penguin Books Ltd, 80 Strand, London WC2R ORL, England
Penguin Group (USA) Inc., 375 Hudson Street, New York, New York 10014, USA
Penguin Group (Canada), 10 Alcorn Avenue, Toronto, Ontario, Canada M4V 3B2
(a division of Pearson Penguin Canada Inc.)
Penguin Ireland, 25 St Stephen's Green, Dublin 2, Ireland
(a division of Penguin Books Ltd)
Penguin Group (Australia), 250 Camberwell Road, Camberwell, Victoria 3124,
Australia (a division of Pearson Australia Group Pty Ltd)
Penguin Books India Pvt Ltd, 11 Community Centre,
Panchsheel Park, New Delhi – 110 017, India
Penguin Group (NZ), cnr Airborne and Rosedale Roads, Albany,
Auckland 1310, New Zealand (a division of Pearson New Zealand Ltd)
Penguin Books (South Africa) (Pty) Ltd, 24 Sturdee Avenue,
Rosebank 2196, South Africa

Penguin Books Ltd, Registered Offices: 80 Strand, London WC2R ORL, England

www.penguin.com

The Early Stories first published in the USA by Alfred A. Knopf, Inc. 2003
First published in Great Britain by Hamish Hamilton 2004
Published in Penguin Books 2005
This selection published as a Pocket Penguin 2005

1

Copyright © John Updike, 2003
All rights reserved

The moral right of the author has been asserted

Set in 10.5/12.5pt Monotype Dante
Typeset by Palimpsest Book Production Limited
Polmont, Stirlingshire
Printed in England by Clays Ltd, St Ives plc

Contents

Author's Note

An author, rereading his own work, is pleased and entertained unpredictably, often outside the confines of other people's favorites – in my case, narratives describing the uneasy pursuit of domestic and erotic happiness in the small towns of the northeastern United States. Rereading the one hundred and three items that went into my recent collection *The Early Stories*, I enjoyed, perhaps more than they deserved, stories derived from trips to exotic realms – tales that deliver, aside from my characters' customary unease, the excitement of adventure into fresh terrains, which seem to promise new possibilities and the freedom to explore those possibilities. The details speak with an intrinsic interest, an interest bordering on the journalistic, and the stories, with so much to vivify, run a bit longer than my usual. Here are three such, distilled from many miles.

Nevada

Poor Culp. His wife, Sarah, wanted to marry her lover as soon as the divorce came through, she couldn't wait a day, the honeymoon suite in Honolulu had been booked six weeks in advance. So Culp, complaisant to the end, agreed to pick the girls up in Reno and drive them back to Denver. He arranged to be in San Francisco on business and rented a car. Over the phone, Sarah mocked his plan – why not fly? An expert in petroleum extraction, he hoped by driving to extract some scenic benefit from domestic ruin. Until they had moved to Denver and their marriage exploded in the thinner atmosphere, they had lived in New Jersey, and the girls had seen little of the West.

He arrived in Reno around five in the afternoon, having detoured south from Interstate 80. The city looked kinder than he had expected. He found the address Sarah had given him, a barn-red boardinghouse behind a motel distinguished by a giant flashing domino. He dreaded yet longed for the pain of seeing Sarah again – divorced, free of him, exultant, about to take wing into a new marriage. But she had taken wing before he arrived. His two daughters were sitting on a tired cowhide sofa, next to an empty desk, like patients in a dentist's anteroom.

Polly, who was eleven, leaped up to greet him. 'Mommy's left,' she said. 'She thought you'd be here hours ago.'

Laura, sixteen, rose with a self-conscious languor from the tired sofa, smoothing her skirt behind, and added, 'Jim was with her. He got really mad when you didn't show.'

Culp apologized. 'I didn't know her schedule was so tight.'

Laura perhaps misheard him, answering, 'Yeah, she was really uptight.'

'I took a little detour to see Lake Tahoe.'

'Oh, Dad,' Laura said. 'You and your sightseeing.'

'Were you worried?' he asked.

'Naa.'

A little woman with a square jaw hopped from a side room behind the empty desk. 'They was good as good, Mr. Culp. Just sat there, wouldn't even take a sandwich I offered to make for no charge. Laura here kept telling the little one, "Don't you be childish, Daddy wouldn't let us down." I'm Betsy Morgan, we've heard of each other but never met officially.' Sarah had mentioned her in her letters: Morgan the pirate, her landlady and residency witness. Fred Culp saw himself through Mrs. Morgan's eyes: cuckold, defendant, discardee. Though her eye was merry, the hand she offered him was dry as a bird's foot.

He could only think to ask, 'How did the proceedings go?'

The question seemed foolish to him, but not to Mrs. Morgan. 'Seven minutes, smooth as silk. Some of these judges, they give a girl a hard time just to keep themselves from being bored. But your Sary stood right up to him. She has that way about her.'

'Yes, she did. Does. More and more. Girls, got your bags?'

'Right behind the sofy here. I would have kept their room one night more, but then this lady from Connecticut showed up yesterday could take it for the six weeks.'

'That's fine. I'll take them someplace with a pool.'

'They'll be missed, I tell you truly,' the landlady said, and she kissed the two girls on their cheeks. This had been a family of sorts, there were real tears in her eyes; but Polly couldn't wait for the hug to pass before blurting to her father,

'We had pool privileges at the Domino, and one time all these Mexicans came and used it for a *bath*room!'

They drove to a motel not the Domino. Laura and he watched Polly swim. 'Laura, don't you want to put on a suit?'

'Naa. Mom made us swim so much I got diver's ear.'

Culp pictured Sarah lying on a poolside chaise longue, in the bikini with the orange and purple splashes. One smooth wet arm was flung up to shield her eyes. Other women noticeably had legs or breasts; Sarah's beauty had been most vivid in her arms, rounded and fine and firm, arms that never aged, without a trace of wobble above the elbow, though at her next birthday she would be forty. Indeed, that was how Sarah had put the need for divorce: she couldn't bear to turn forty with him. As if then you began a return journey that could not be broken.

Laura was continuing, 'Also, Dad, if you *must* know, it's that time of the month.'

With clumsy jubilance, Polly hurled her body from the rattling board and surfaced grinning through the kelp of her own hair. She climbed from the pool and slapfooted to his side, shivering. 'Want to walk around and play the slots?' Goose bumps had erected the white hairs on her thighs into a ghostly halo. 'Want to? It's fun.'

Laura intervened maternally. 'Don't *make* him, Polly. Daddy's tired and depressed.'

'Who says? Let's go. I may never see Reno again.' The city, as they walked, reminded him of New Jersey's little municipalities. The desert clarity at evening had the even steel glint of industrial haze. Above drab shop fronts, second-story windows proclaimed residence with curtains and a flowerpot. There were churches, which he hadn't expected. And a river, a trickling shadow of the Passaic, flowed through. The courthouse, Mecca to so many, seemed too modest; it wore the dogged granite dignity of justice the country over. Only the Reno downtown, garish as a carnival midway, was different. Polly led him to doors she was forbidden to enter and gave him nickels to play for her inside. She loved the slot machines, loved them for their fruity colors and their sleepless glow and their sudden gush of release, jingling, lighting, as luck struck now here, now there, across the dark casino. Feeling the silky heave of their guts as he fed the slot and pulled the handle, rewarded a few times with the delicious spitting of coins into the troughs other hands had smoothed to his touch, Culp came to love them, too; he and Polly made a gleeful, hopeful pair, working their way from casino to casino, her round face pressed to the window so she could see him play, and the plums jerk into being, and the bells and cherries do their waltz of chance, 1–2–3. One place was wide open to the sidewalk. A grotesquely large machine stood ready for silver dollars.

Polly said, 'Mommy won twenty dollars on that one once.'

Culp asked Laura, who had trailed after them in disdainful silence, 'Was Jim with you the whole time?'

'No, he only came the last week.' She searched her father's face for what he wanted to know. 'He stayed at the Domino.'

Polly drew close to listen. Culp asked her, 'Did you like Jim?'

Her eyes with difficulty shifted from visions of mechanical delight. 'He was too serious. He said the slots were a racket and they wouldn't get a penny of his.'

Laura said, 'I thought he was an utter *pill*, Dad.'

'You don't have to think that to please me.'

'He *was*. I told her, too.'

'You shouldn't have. Listen, it's her life, not yours.' On the hospital-bright sidewalk, both his girls' faces looked unwell, stricken. Culp put a silver dollar into the great machine, imagining that something of Sarah had rubbed off here and that through this electric ardor she might speak to him. But the machine's size was unnatural; the guts felt sluggish, spinning. A plum, a bar, a star. No win. Turning, he resented that Polly and Laura, still staring, seemed stricken for *him*.

Laura said, 'Better come eat, Dad. We'll show you a place where they have pastrami like back east.'

As Route 40 poured east, Nevada opened into a strange no-color – a rusted gray, or the lavender that haunts the corners of overexposed color slides. The Humboldt River, which had sustained the pioneer caravans, shadowed the expressway, tinting its valley with a dull green that fed dottings of cattle. But for the cattle, and the cars that brushed by him as if he were doing thirty and not eighty miles an hour, and an occasional gas station and cabin café promising SLOTS, there was little sign of life in Nevada. This pleased Culp; it enabled him to run off in peace the home movies of Sarah stored in his head. Sarah pushing the lawn mower in the South Orange back yard. Sarah pushing a blue baby carriage, English, with little white wheels, around the fountain in Washington Square. Sarah, not yet his wife, waiting for him in a brown-and-green peasant skirt under the marquee of a movie house on Fifty-seventh Street. Sarah, a cool suburban hostess in chalk-pink sack dress, easing through their jammed living room with a platter of parsleyed egg halves. Sarah after a party, drunk in a black lace bra, doing the Twist at the foot of their bed. Sarah in blue jeans crying out that it was nobody's *fault*, that there was nothing he could *do*, just let her *alone*; and hurling a quarter-pound of butter across the kitchen, so the calendar fell off the wall. Sarah in miniskirt leaving their house in Denver for a date, just like a teenager, the sprinkler on their flat front lawn spinning in the evening cool. Sarah trim and sardonic at the marriage counsellor's, under the pressed-paper panelling where the man had hung not only his diplomas but his Aspen skiing medals. Sarah some Sunday long ago raising the shades to wake him, light flooding her translucent nightgown. Sarah lifting her sudden eyes to him at some table, some moment, somewhere, in conspiracy – he hadn't known he had taken so many reels, they just kept coming in his head. Nevada beautifully, emptily poured by. The map was full of ghost towns. Laura sat beside him, reading the map. 'Dad, here's a town called Nixon.'

'Let's go feel sorry for it.'

'You passed it. It was off the road after Sparks. The next real town is Lovelock.'

'What's real about it?'

'Should you be driving so fast?'

In the back seat, Polly struggled with her needs. 'Can we stop in the next real town to eat?'

Culp said, 'You should have eaten more breakfast.'

'I hate hash browns.'

'But you like bacon.'

'The hash browns had touched it.'

Laura said, 'Polly, stop bugging Daddy, you're making him nervous.'

Culp told her, 'I am *not* nervous.'

Polly told her, 'I can't keep holding it.'

'Baby. You just went less than an hour ago.'

'I'm nervous.'

Culp laughed. Laura said, 'You're not funny. You're not a baby any more.'

Polly said, 'Yeah, and you're not a wife, either.'

Silence.

'Nobody said I was.'

Nevada spun by. Sarah stepped out of a car, their old

Corvair convertible, wearing a one-piece bathing suit. Her hair was stiff and sun-bleached and wild. She was eating a hot dog loaded with relish. Culp looked closer and there was sand in her ear, as in a delicate discovered shell.

Polly announced, 'Dad, that sign said a place in three miles. "Soft Drinks, Sandwiches, Beer, Ice, and Slots."'

'Slots, slots,' Laura spat, furious for a reason that eluded her father. 'Slots and sluts, that's all there is in this dumb state.'

Culp asked, 'Didn't you enjoy Reno?'

'I hated it. What I hated especially was Mom acting on the make all the time.'

'On the make,' 'sluts' – the language of women living together, it occurred to him, coarsens like that of men in the Army. He mildly corrected, 'I'm sure she wasn't on the make, she was just happy to be rid of me.'

'Don't kid yourself, Dad. She was on the make. Even with Jim about to show up she was.'

'Yeah, well,' Polly said, 'you weren't that pure yourself, showing off for that Mexican boy.'

'I wasn't showing off for any bunch of spics, I was practicing my diving, and I suggest you do the same, you toad. You look like a sick frog, the way you go off the board. A sick *fat* frog.'

'Yeah, well. Mommy said you weren't so thin at my age yourself.'

Culp intervened: 'It's *nice* to be plump at your age. Otherwise, you won't have anything to shape up when you're Laura's age.'

Polly giggled, scandalized. Laura said, 'Don't flirt, Dad,' and crossed her thighs; she was going to be one of those women, Culp vaguely saw, who have legs. She smoothed back the hair from her brow in a gesture that tripped the home-movie camera again: Sarah before the mirror. He could have driven forever this way; if he had known Nevada was so easy, he could have planned to reach the Utah line, or detoured north to some ghost towns. But they had made reservations in Elko, and stopped there.

The motel was more of a hotel, four stories high; on the ground floor, a cavernous dark casino glimmered with the faces of the slots and the shiny uniforms of the change girls. Though it was only three in the afternoon, Culp wanted to go in there, to get a drink at the bar, where the bottles glowed like a row of illumined stalagmites. But his daughters, after inspecting their rooms, dragged him out into the sunshine. Elko was a flat town, full of space, as airy with emptiness as an old honeycomb. The broad street in front of the hotel held railroad tracks in its center. To Polly's amazed delight, a real train – nightmarish in scale but docile in manner – materialized on these tracks, halted, ruminated, and then ponderously, thoughtfully dragged westward its chuckling infinity of freight cars. They walked down broad sunstruck sidewalks, past a drunken Indian dressed in clothes as black as his shadow, to a museum of mining. Polly coveted the glinting nuggets, Laura yawned before a case of old-fashioned barbed wire and sought her reflection in the glass. Culp came upon an exhibit, between Indian beads and pioneer hardware, incongruously devoted to Thomas Alva Edison. He and Sarah and the girls, driving home through the peppery stenches of carbon waste and butane from a Sunday on the beach at Point Pleasant, would pass a service island on the Jersey Turnpike named for Edison. They would stop for supper at another one, named for Joyce Kilmer. The hot tar on the parking lot would slightly yield beneath their rubber flip-flops. Sarah would go in for her hot dog wearing her dashiki beach wrapper – hip-length, with slits for her naked arms. These lovely arms would be

8

burned pink in the crooks. The sun would have ignited a conflagration of clouds beyond the great retaining tanks. Here, in Elko, the sun rested gently on the overexposed purple of the ridges around them. On the highest ridge a large letter *E* had been somehow cut, or inset, in what seemed limestone. Polly asked why.

He answered, 'I suppose for airplanes.'

Laura amplified, 'If they don't put initials up, the pilots can't tell the towns apart, they're all so boring.'

'I like Elko,' Polly said. 'I wish we lived here.'

'Yeah, what would Daddy do for a living?'

This was hard. In real life, he was a chemical engineer for a conglomerate that was planning to exploit Colorado shale. Polly said, 'He could fix slot machines and then at night come back in disguise and play them so they'd pay him lots of money.'

Both girls, it seemed to Culp, had forgotten that he would not be living with them in their future, that this peaceful dusty nowhere was an exception to the rule. He took Polly's hand, crossing the railroad tracks, though the tracks were arrow-straight and no train was materializing between here and the horizon.

Laura flustered him by taking his arm as they walked into the dining room, which was beyond the dark grotto of slots. The waitress slid an expectant glance at the child, after he had ordered a drink for himself. 'No. She's only sixteen.'

When the waitress had gone, Laura told him, 'Everybody says I look older than sixteen; in Reno with Mom, I used to wander around in the places and nobody ever said anything. Except one old fart who told me they'd put him in jail if I didn't go away.'

Polly asked, 'Daddy, when're you going to play the slots?'

'I thought I'd wait till after dinner.'

'That's too long.'

'O.K., I'll play now. Just until the salad comes.' He took a mouthful of his drink, pushed up from the table, and fed ten quarters into a machine that Polly could watch. Though he won nothing, being there, amid the machines' warm and fantastic colors, consoled him. Experimenting, he pressed the button marked CHANGE. A girl in a red uniform crinkling like embers came to his side inquisitively. Her face, though not old, had the Western dryness – eyes smothered in charcoal, mouth tightened as if about to say, *I thought so*. But something sturdy and hollow-backed in her stance touched Culp with an intuition. It was a little like oil extraction: you just sensed it, below the surface. Her uniform's devilish cut bared her white arms to the shoulder. He gave her a five-dollar bill to change into quarters. The waitress was bringing the salad. Heavy in one pocket, he returned to the table.

'Poor Dad,' Laura volunteered. 'That prostitute really turned him on.'

'Laura, I'm not sure you know what a prostitute is.'

'Mom said every woman is a prostitute, one way or another.'

'You know your mother exaggerates.'

'I know she's a bitch, you mean.'

'Laura.'

'She *is*, Dad. Look what she's done to you. Now she'll do it to Jim.'

'You and I have different memories of your mother. You don't remember her when you were little.'

'I don't want to live with her, either. When we all get back to Denver, I want to live with *you*. If she and I live together, it'll always be competing, that's how it was in Reno; who needs it? When *I* get to forty, I'm going to tell my lover to shoot me.'

Polly cried out – an astonishing noise, like the crash of a jackpot. '*Stop* it,' she told Laura. 'Stop talking big. That's all you do, is talk big.' The child, salad dressing gleaming on her chin, pushed her voice toward her sister through tears: 'You want Mommy and Daddy to fight all the time instead of love each other even though they *are* divorced.'

With an amused smile, Laura turned her back on Polly's outburst and patted Culp's arm. 'Poor Dad,' she said. 'Poor old Dad.'

Their steaks came, and Polly's tears dried. They walked out into Elko again and at the town's one movie theater saw a Western. Burt Lancaster, a downtrodden Mexican, after many insults, including crucifixion, turned implacable avenger and killed nine hirelings of a racist rancher. Polly seemed to be sleeping through the bloodiest parts. They walked back through the dry night to the hotel. Their two adjoining rooms each held twin beds. Laura's suitcase had appeared on the bed beside his.

Culp said, 'You better sleep with your sister.'

'Why? We'll have the door between open, in case she has nightmares.'

'I want to read.'

'So do I.'

'You go to sleep now. We're going to make Salt Lake tomorrow.'

'Big thrill. Dad, she mumbles and kicks her covers all the time.'

'Do as I say, love. I'll stay here reading until you're asleep.'

'And then what?'

'I may go down and have another drink.'

Her expression reminded him of how, in the movie, the villain had looked when Burt Lancaster showed that he, too, had a gun. Culp lay on the bedspread reading a pamphlet they had bought at the museum, about ghost towns; champagne and opera sets had been transported up the valleys, where now not a mule survived. Train whistles at intervals scooped long pockets from the world beyond his room. The breathing from the other room had fallen level. He tiptoed in and saw them both asleep, his daughters. Laura had been reading a book about the persecution of the Indians and now it lay beside her hand, with its childish short fingernails. Relaxed, her face revealed its freckles, its plumpness, the sorrowing stretched smoothness of the closed lids. Polly's face wore a film of night sweat on her brow; his kiss came away tasting salty. He did not kiss Laura, in case she was faking. He switched off the light and stood considering what he must do. A train howled on the other side of the wall. The beautiful emptiness of Nevada, where he might never be again, sucked at the room like a pump.

Downstairs, his intuition was borne out. The change girl had noticed him, and said now, 'How's it going?'

'Fair. You ever go off duty?'

'What's duty?'

He waited at the bar, waiting for the bourbon to fill him; it couldn't, the room inside him kept expanding, and when she joined him, after one o'clock, sidling up on the stool (a cowboy moved over) in a taut cotton dress that hid the tops of her arms, the blur on her face seemed a product of her inner chemistry, not his. 'You've a room?' As she asked him that, her jaw went square: Mrs. Morgan in a younger version.

'I do,' he said, 'but it's full of little girls.'

She reached for his bourbon and sipped and said, in a voice older than her figure, 'This place is lousy with rooms.'

Culp arrived back in his own room after four. He must have been noisier than he thought, for a person in a white nightgown appeared in the connecting doorway. Culp could not see her features, she was a good height, she reminded him of nobody. Good. From the frozen pose of her, she was scared – scared of him. Good.

'Dad?'

'Yep.'

'You O.K.?'

'Sure.' Though already he could feel the morning sun's grinding on his temples. 'You been awake, sweetie? I'm sorry.'

'I was worried about you.' But Laura did not cross the threshold into his room.

'Very worried?'

'Naa.'

'Listen. It's not your job to take care of me. It's my job to take care of you.'

Ethiopia

The Addis Ababa Hilton has a lobby of cool and lustrous stone and a giant, heated, cruciform swimming pool. The cross-shape is plain from the balconies of the ninth-floor rooms, from which also one can see the long white façade of the Emperor's palace. In the other direction, there are acres of tin shacks, and a church on a hill like the nipple on a breast of dust. Emerging from the pool, which feels like layers of rapidly tearing silk, one shivers uncontrollably until dry, though the sun is brilliant, and the sky diamond-pure. The land is high, and the air not humid. One dries quickly. The elevators are swift and silent. From the high floors the white umbrellas on the restaurant tables beside the pool make a rosary of perfect circles. All this is true. What is not true is that Prester John doubles as the desk clerk, and the Queen of Sheba manages the glass-walled gift shop, wherein one can buy tight-woven baskets of multicolored straw, metal mirrors, and Coptic crosses of carved wood costing thousands of Ethiopian dollars, which relate to the American dollar as seven to three.

The young American couple arrived at the hotel very tired, having been ten days in Kenya, where they had seen and photographed lions, leopards, cheetahs, hyraxes, oryxes, dik-diks, steinboks, klipspringers, oribis, topis, kudus, impalas, elands, Thomson's gazelles, Grant's gazelles, hartebeests, wildebeests, waterbucks, bushbucks, zebras, giraffes, flamingos, marabou storks, Masai warriors, baboons, elephants, warthogs, and rhinoceroses – everything hoped for, indeed, except hippos. There had been one asleep in a

ool in the Ngorongoro Crater, but it had looked too much
ike a rock to photograph, and the young man of the
American couple had passed it by, confident there would be
nore. There never were. It had been his only chance to get
a hippopotamus on film. Prester John, cool behind his desk
of lustrous green marble, divined this, and efficiently, gratu-
tously arranged that they spend the night away from Addis
Ababa, in the Ethiopian countryside. The countryside was
ight brown. Distant figures swathed in white trod the tan
andscape with the floating step of men trying to steady
hemselves on a trampoline. But these were women, all
beautiful. The beauty of their black faces, glimpsed, lashed
he windows of the car like fistfuls of thrown sand. Some
carried yellow parasols. Some led white donkeys. A few rode
n rubber-wheeled carts, rickety and polychrome, their
mouths and nostrils veiled against the dust. He tried to
photograph these women, but they turned their heads, and
he results would come out blurred.

The hotel was cushioned in bougainvillea and stuffed with
Germans. At six o'clock a bus took all the Germans away and
he young Americans became the only guests. They walked the
blossoming grounds, and looked from their balcony to
he brown lake distilled from the tan landscape by a cement
dam, and in their room read magazines taken from the hotel
obby – *Ce Soir, Il Tempo, Sturm und Drang*, the English edition
of the official monthly publication of the Polish Chamber of
Commerce, the annual handbook of Yugoslavian soccer, the
quarterly journal of the Australian Dermatology Association
(incorporating *Tasmanian Hides*). 'God, I love this country,'
he announced aloud, letting his magazine sink beside him to
the bed.

'Quiet,' she said. 'I'm reading.' The Brazilian edition of
Newsweek.

'If you ever get tired of reading,' he began.

'It's too hot,' she said.

'Really? Actually, as evening comes on, in these high, dry countries –'

'Have it your way, then,' she said, noisily turning a tissue thin page. 'It's too cold.'

There was a knock on the door. It was their driver, asking in his excellent English if they wanted to see the hippopotami before dinner. Yes, they did. Their limousine wound through low, menacing foliage to a sluggish brown river. It seemed empty and scarcely flowing. They walked along a dim path beside the riverbank and met Prester John, barefoot, in rags and carrying a staff. Though he seemed a shade darker than in his hotel uniform, he was recognizably the same man – small, clever, with beautiful feminine hands and a hurt, monkish, liverish look beneath his eyes. He looked, she thought, like Sammy Davis, Jr.; but, then, so many men in Ethiopia look like Sammy Davis, Jr. Prester John led them to a shaggy point above the river and made a noise of sonorous chuckling deep in his throat – deeper than his throat; his entire body and belly thrummed and resonated with the noise. And then in the dusk little snags appeared in the river current: hippopotamus eyes. As the Americans grew accustomed to the dusk, and the dusk to them, to the eyes were added ears and the tops of heads appeared above the water, and the bulbous immensity of a back arched upward into a dive. I was a family, a clan, with two babies among them, all calling to one another; their deep soft snorting continued underwater as an unheard, vibrating jubilance. The air became as full of it as the river, one brown world flooded with familial snorting, until the hippopotami had tugged themselves around the bend and into night. Prester John accepted his tip with a bow and the shadow of a genuflexion. The driver was relieved to

ind his car unharmed in the bushes. Back at the hotel, the
oung American couple were served dinner in solitary splen-
lor. Unseen hands had prepared a banquet; for all its eerie
solation, the meal was delicious. He wondered how the hotel
urned a profit. He thought of sharing the question with his
oride, but kept silent. Oh, if only he knew how to talk to her!
The silence between them grated the plates and made the
ilver clash with the fury of swords. His thoughts moved on,
o the hippos. If only there had been a notch or two more
ight! Oh, if only he had brought a longer lens!

3ack in Addis, Prester John perceived that they were bored,
and arranged to have a party thrown for them. He himself
was the host; the Queen of Sheba was the hostess. Her hair
was up in the halo of an Afro, and as she moved in her robe
of all possible colors her body tapped now here, now there.
The rings on her fingers formed a hoard and the little gold
circles of her granny glasses gave her eyes a monkish humor.
Her blackness was the shade in which God had designed
Adam and Eve, a color from which the young American
couple felt their own whiteness as a catastrophic falling off,
caused helter-skelter by the Northern clime, snow, wolves,
camouflage, and the survival of the fittest. The Queen of
Sheba introduced them to beautiful, static people whose titles
of courtesy were Ato, Woizero, and Woizerit. A Woizerit was
unmarried. It seemed an elaborate way to say it. Also elabo-
rately, the Emperor was never referred to but as His Imperial
Majesty, which became HIM.

'. . . until we are rid of HIM . . .'

'. . . the latest story about HIM . . .'

'I understand,' the young American said to a stately
Woizerit who had studied three years at the University of
Iowa, 'you're in television.'

Prester John gracefully interceded. 'This lovely lady,' he said, '*is* Ethiopian television.' His magical feminine hand turned a dial, and there she was, giving news about the latest Palestinian hijacking.

'Hitler,' a swarthy but handsome gentleman was telling the young American wife, 'had the correct idea but was not permitted to complete it. A vivid proof of God's non-existence.'

'Suppose I told you,' she said, 'I was Jewish?'

He surveyed her face, and then her blond body, lovingly 'It would not lessen,' he told her, 'my reverence for Hitler. But reverence for her was what he expressed, for he clung pinchingly to her arm as if she had consented to join him in some superb indecency.

Her husband had found a fellow-American, a pale-brown Black woman from Detroit, in the pay of the American Embassy. They huddled close together, sharing remembrance of that remote exotic land of Lincoln Continentals and Drake's Cakes. 'You happy here?' he asked at last.

'It'll do,' she said, shrugging and, obliged to elaborate on the shrug, adding, 'I can't get servants. They're very polite and I offer top dollar, but the Ethiopians will not work for me.'

'But why not?'

Seeing that he truly didn't know, very graciously she made a little gesture as if parting curtains, disclosing – herself. Seeing that he still didn't know, she elaborated, 'They have this racial hang-up. They keep telling you how Semitic they are.'

The Queen of Sheba clapped her hands imperiously. No Westerner could have produced that sound, as if with blocks of wood: worlds of body language are being lost. The guests sat to eat around great multicolored baskets lined with a delicious rubbery bread. One ate by tearing off pieces and seizing food as if picking up coals with a pot holder. The young Americans were delighted to be engaging in a custom. Prester John admired their pragmatism. His voice was high, reedy, and not accidentally unpleasant. 'I would not want to say,' he said, 'the many negative things I could say about America. But you have done this one thing of genius. The credit card. Money without money. That is a thing truly revolutionary. The world is thus transformed, while the political philosophers amuse one another.'

'Is that what you do? I mean, are you a political scientist? A teacher?' The American was not sure this was still Prester John – he seemed frailer, edgier.

'What do I do? I read Proust, over and over. And I write.'

'Could I read your books?' the American wife chimed in, from across the basket, at whose rim the admirer of Hitler was showing her how to eat raw meat, an Ethiopian delicacy.

'No,' was the response, said caressingly. 'In Ethiopia, there is no publishing.'

'You understand,' the television Woizerit murmured on the American's other side. 'HIM.'

'I write and I write,' the frail clever host elaborated, 'and then I read it all aloud to one special friend. And then I destroy it. All.'

'How terrible. Is that friend here?'

'No.' He smiled, forming a little prayer tent with his hands. He was certainly Prester John. A medieval face twitched in his midnight skin. 'Do not eat raw meat. The uninitiated vomit for days.' He relaxed, slumped in his gaudy robes. 'Yes.' His voice went high again, reedy, mockingly informative. 'In this ancient kingdom, misplaced to Africa, we have been compelled to raise the art of living to the point of the tenuous.'

Though the party was gathering strength, the young Americans were tired. The Queen of Sheba and Prester John insisted on accompanying them back to the hotel, since marauders roam the slums with impunity; the poverty is acute despite massive infusions of American aid, corruption and reaction reign here as everywhere save China, not even one's driver of twenty years' service can be trusted, terrorists on behalf of Eritrean independence are ubiquitous. A curious optical effect: in the darkness within the car, the two legendary Ethiopians disappeared but for their clothes, which rustled with utmost courtesy, and but for their words, paraphrased above. Nevertheless, a disturbing and flattering possibility, indecent yet not impractical, communicated itself to the minds of their guests, as through layers of fluttering, tearing silk. In the cool lobby their shouted farewells echoed of disappointment. Oh, what *was* the custom?

In his twin bed on the ninth floor, the man of the young couple thought, The Queen of Sheba, black yet not Black, boyoboyoboy. Mine, she could be mine, as the darkness inside me is mine, as the spangled night sky is mine. God, I love this country. The jewels. The arid height. The Hilton corridors of greenish stone. The tiny dried-up Emperor. The bracing sense of never having been colonized by any European power. How long and lustrous her ebony limbs would feel in the darkness. But I might disappoint her. I might feel lost in her. She might mock me. My sickly pallor. My Free World hang-ups. Better simply snap her picture when she undresses. But the flash batteries died in the Serengeti, that night by the water hole. Darn it! Her breasts. Armpits. Belly. Down, down he is led from one dusky thought to the next. Travel is so sexy. Would the granny glasses come off first, or last?

And beside him his fair wife on her twin bed thinks of airplanes. She dreads flying, especially in Ethiopia, with its high escarpments, small national budget, daredevil pilots trained by Alitalia. Perhaps, if she slept with Prester John, by one of his miracles he could prevent her plane from crashing. Sleeping with men, especially black men, more fancy than fact, if they gave women decent educations they could think about something else. But still . . . His wicked ascetic smile and look of monkish sorrow did cut into her. In the car, his touch, or a fold of his silken robe, accidentally? If he could guarantee on a stack of Bibles the plane wouldn't crash . . . The dedicated hijackers with stockings over their faces, the sudden revolver shots from the security guards disguised as Lebanese businessmen, the rush of air, the lurch above the clouds, the inane patter of the brave stewardesses, the lurid burst of flame from the port engine, the long slow nightmare fall, the mile-wide splash of char on the earth, the scattered suitcases . . . Oh God yes, I'll do anything you want, consider me your slave, your toy. For without life how can there be virtue?

Because of security checks, one must appear at the airport two and a half hours before scheduled departure time. The young American is in the glass-walled hotel shop, dickering with the Queen of Sheba for a Coptic cross. He has reduced her price to fourteen hundred Ethiopian dollars, which is no longer divisible by seven in his head, because of the most recent American dollar devaluation. Fourteen hundred divided by two and one-third minus a little . . . She is bored. The Queen of Sheba thrusts a retractable ballpoint into her towering teased coiffure, and her ebony fingers drum with surprising percussive effect on a glass case. Her nose is straight, her nostrils are narrow. She sighs. These Americans, rendered insubstantial by rising gold, like drops of water running from the back of an aroused crocodile. He asks, will she accept a credit card?

Prester John appears, in shabby livery, with the young American wife in tow. She is flushed, pink, sleepy. Though the lobby is cool, blond ringlets cling to her brow. Hurry, the clever little black man says, you must see the monastery, there is just time before the airplane, it has been arranged.

Trailing protests like dust, the young American is led through the lobby, away from his luggage. It is not the usual limousine this time but a little red Fiat. Prester John does not seem to understand the gears. As he grapples with them, he looks comically like Sammy Davis, Jr. They head out of the city, uphill; the paved road becomes dirt. Prester John gossips nervously about the Queen of Sheba. 'She is a magnificent woman, but thoroughly Oriental. I enjoy her loyalty, yet am vexed by, how shall I say, the lack of *stereo* in her sensibility. She cannot lift her thoughts above jewelry, lechery, and airbases. My intention was to irradiate her with Christian faith, fresh, even raw, from the desert Fathers – to make, here, upon this plateau, a dream to solace the tormented sleep of Europe. Instead, she has made of it something impossibly heavy, a mere fact, like the Catholicism of Ireland, or the Communism of Albania.' He cannot move the gearshift above second gear, so thus roaring they proceed up a dirt road transected by ridges of rock like the backs of sleeping hippopotami. At first, clouds of people in white had rimmed the roadway; now they meet, and swerve to avoid, intermittent donkeys and women staggering beneath wide bundles of little trees. One of these women, bent double like a scorpion, in rags, her feet bare, with long, dark heels and pale, cracked soles, looks familiar; the American turns in his seat. Dust obscures his view. He is certain only that she was not wearing her granny glasses.

Prester John sweats, embarrassed. The road is all rocks now, tan, with a white dusting. 'I am growing worried,' he confesses, 'about your airplane. It is possible I underestimated the difficulty.' He stops the car where the view falls away on one side. The Hilton pool twinkles like a dim star far below them. On the other side, stony sere pastures mount to a copse of viridian trees. Between the trees peep ruddy hints of a long wall. That is the monastery. 'Perhaps,' Prester John offers nervously, 'a photograph? I am profoundly sorry; the road, and these recalcitrant gears . . .'

What the young American sees through his finder looks exactly like the sepia illustrations in his Sunday-school Bible. He sets the lens at infinity and snaps the shutter. But his inward attention is upon his wife, for her calmness, as their next airplane flight draws nearer, puzzles him. Prester John grindingly backs the Fiat around and hurtles downward along the cruel road of rocks; she lightly smiles and with dusty fingertips brushes back the hair from her drying brow. She feels she is already on the airplane – all of Ethiopia is an airplane, thousands of feet above sea level; and it cannot crash. This is true.

I Am Dying, Egypt, Dying

Clem came from Buffalo and spoke in the neutral American accent that sends dictionary makers there. His pronunciation was clear and colorless, his manners were impeccable, his clothes freshly laundered and appropriate no matter where he was, however far from home. Rich and unmarried, he travelled a lot; he had been to Athens and Rio, Las Vegas and Hong Kong, Leningrad and Sydney, and now Cairo. His posture was perfect, but he walked without swing; people at first liked him, because his apparent perfection reflected flatteringly upon them, and then distrusted him, because his perfection disclosed no flaw. As he travelled, he studied the guidebooks conscientiously, picked up words of the local language, collected prints and artifacts. He was serious but not humorless; indeed, his smile, a creeping but finally complete revelation of utterly even and white front teeth, with a bit of tongue flirtatiously pinched between them, was one of the things that led people on, that led them to hope for the flaw, the entering crack. There were hopeful signs. At the bar he took one drink too many, the hurried last drink that robs the dinner wine of taste. Though he enjoyed human society, he couldn't dance, politely refusing always.

He had a fine fair square-shouldered body, surely masculine and yet somehow neutral, which he solicitously covered with oil against the sun that, as they moved up the Nile, grew sharper and more tropical. He fell asleep in deck chairs, uncannily immobile, glistening, as the two riverbanks at their

24

safe distance glided by – date palms, taut green fields irri-
gated by rotating donkeys, pyramids of white round pots,
trapezoidal houses of elephant-colored mud, mud-colored
children silently waving, and the roseate desert cliffs beyond,
massive parentheses. Glistening like a mirror, he slept in this
gliding parenthesis with a godlike calm that possessed the
landscape, transformed it into a steady dreaming. Clem said
of himself, awaking, apologizing, smiling with that bit of
pinched tongue, that he slept badly at night, suffered from
insomnia. This also was a hopeful sign. People wanted to
love him.

There were not many on the boat. The Six-Day War had
discouraged tourists. Indeed, at Nag Hammadi they did pass
under a bridge in which Israeli commandos had blasted three
neat but not very conclusive holes; some wooden planks had
been laid on top and the traffic of carts and rickety lorries
continued. And at Aswan they saw anti-aircraft batteries
defending the High Dam. For the cruise, the war figured as
a luxurious amount of space on deck and a pleasant dispro-
portion between the seventy crewmen and the twenty paying
passengers. These twenty were:

Three English couples, middle-aged but for one miniskirted
wife, who was thought for days to be a daughter.

Two German boys; they wore bathing trunks to all the
temples, yet seemed to know the gods by name and perhaps
were future archaeologists.

A French couple, in their sixties. The man had been
tortured in World War II; his legs were unsteady, and his spine
had fused in a curve. He moved over the desert rubble and
uneven stairways with tiny shuffling steps and studied the
murals by means of a mirror hung around his neck. Yet he,
too, knew the gods and would murmur worshipfully.

Three Egyptians, a man and two women, in their thirties,

of a professional class, teachers or museum curators, cosmopolitan and handsome, given to laughter among themselves, even while the guide, a cherubic old Bedouin called Poppa Omar, was lecturing.

A fluffy and sweet, ample and perfumed American widow and her escort, a short bald native of New Jersey who for fifteen years had run tours in Africa, armed with a fancy fly whisk and an impenetrable rudeness toward natives of the continent.

A small-time travelogue-maker from Green Bay working his way south to Cape Town with a hundred pounds of photographic equipment.

A stocky blond couple, fortyish, who kept to themselves, hired their own guides, and were presumed to be Russian.

A young Scandinavian woman, beautiful, alone.

Clem.

Clem had joined the cruise at the last minute; he had been in Amsterdam and become oppressed by the low sky and tight-packed houses, the cold canal touring boats and the bad Indonesian food and the prostitutes illuminated in their windows like garish great candy. He had flown to Cairo and not liked it better. A cheeseburger in the Hilton offended him by being gamy: a goatburger. In the plaza outside, a man rustled up to him and asked if he had had any love last night. The city, with its incessant twinkle of car horns and furtive-eyed men in pajamas, seemed unusable, remote. The museum was full of sandbags. The heart of King Tut's treasure had been hidden in case of invasion; but his gold sarcophagus, feathered in lapis lazuli and carnelian, did touch Clem, with its hint of death, of flight, of floating. A pamphlet in the Hilton advertised a six-day trip on the Nile, Luxor north to Abydos, back to Luxor, and on south to Aswan, in a luxurious boat. It sounded passive and educational, which appealed to Clem; he had gone to college at the University of Rochester and felt a need to keep rounding off his education, to bring it up to Ivy League standards. Also, the tan would look great back in Buffalo.

Stepping from the old DC-3 at the Luxor airport, he was smitten by the beauty of the desert, rose-colored and motionless around him. His element, perhaps. What was his travelling, his bachelorhood, but a search for his element? He was thirty-four and still seemed to be merely visiting the world. Even in Buffalo, walking the straight shaded streets where he had played as a small boy, entering the homes and restaurants where he was greeted by name, sitting in the two-room office where he put in the hour or two of telephoning that managed the parcel of securities and property fallen to him from his father's death, he felt somehow light – limited to forty-four pounds of luggage, dressed with the unnatural rigor people assume at the outset of a trip. A puff of air off Lake Erie and he would be gone, and the city, with its savage blustery winters, its deep-set granite mansions, its factories, its iron bison in the railroad terminal, would not have noticed. He would leave only his name in gilt paint on a list of singles tennis champions above the bar of his country club. But he knew he had been a methodical, joyless player to watch, a back-courter too full of lessons to lose.

He knew a lot about himself: he knew that this lightness, the brittle unmarred something he carried, was his treasure, which his demon willed him to preserve. Stepping from the airplane at Luxor, he had greeted his demon in the air – air ideally clean, dry as a mirror. From the window of his cabin he sensed again, in the glittering width of the Nile – much bluer than he had expected – and in the unflecked alkaline sky and in the tapestry strip of anciently worked green between them, that he would be happy for this trip. He liked sunning on the deck that first afternoon. Only the Scandinavian girl, in an orange bikini, kept him company. Both were silent. The boat was still tied up at the Luxor dock, a flight of stone steps; a few yards away, across a gulf of water and paved banking, a traffic of peddlers and cart drivers stared across. Clem liked that gulf and liked it when the boat cast loose and began gliding between the fields, the villages, the desert. He liked the first temples: gargantuan Karnak, its pillars upholding the bright blank sky; gentler Luxor, with its built-in mosque and its little naked queen touching her king's giant calf; Hollywoodish Dendera – its restored roofs had brought in darkness and dampness and bats that moved on the walls like intelligent black gloves.

Clem even, at first, liked the peddlers. Tourist-starved, they touched him in their hunger, thrusting scarabs and old coins and clay mummy dolls at him, moaning and grunting English: 'How much? How much you give me? Very fine. Fifty. Both. Take both. Both for thirty-five.' Clem peeked down, caught his eye on a turquoise glint, and wavered; his mother liked keepsakes and he had friends in Buffalo who would be amused. Into this flaw, this tentative crack of interest, they stuffed more things, strange sullied objects salvaged from the desert, alabaster vases, necklaces of mummy heads. Their brown hands probed and rubbed; their faces looked stunned, unblinking, as if, under the glaring sun, they were conducting business in the dark. Indeed, some did have eyes whitened by trachoma. Hoping to placate them with a purchase, Clem bargained for the smallest thing he could see, a lapis-lazuli bug the size of a fingernail. 'Ten, then,' the old peddler said, irritably making the 'give me' gesture with his palm. Holding his wallet high, away from their hands, Clem leafed through the big notes for the absurdly small five-piaster bills, tattered and fragile with use. The purchase, amounting to little more

han a dime, excited the peddlers; ignoring the other tourists,
hey multiplied and crowded against him. Something warm
and hard was inserted into his hand, his other sleeve was
plucked, his pockets were patted, and he wheeled, his tongue
pinched between his teeth flirtatiously. It was a nightmare;
he dream thought crossed his mind that he might be
scratched, marred.

He broke away and rejoined the other tourists in the sanc-
tum of a temple courtyard. One of the Egyptian women
came up to him and said, 'I do not mean to remonstrate, but
you are torturing them by letting them see all those fifties
and hundreds in your wallet.'

'I'm sorry.' He blushed like a scolded schoolboy. 'I just
didn't want to be rude.'

'You must be. There is no question of hurt feelings. You
are the man in the moon to them. They have no compre-
hension of your charm.'

The strange phrasing of her last sentence, expressing not
quite what she meant, restored his edge and dulled her
rebuke. She was the shorter and the older of the two Egyptian
women; her eyes were green and there was an earnest
mischief, a slight pressure, in her upward glance. Clem
relaxed, almost slouching. 'The sad part is, some of their
things, I'd rather like to buy.'

'Then do,' she said, and walked away, her hips swinging.
So a move had been made. He had expected it to come from
the Scandinavian girl.

That evening the Egyptian trio invited him to their table in
the bar. The green-eyed woman said, 'I hope I was not scold-
ing. I did not mean to remonstrate, merely to inform.'

'Of course,' Clem said. 'Listen. I was being plucked to
death. I needed rescuing.'

'Those men,' the Egyptian man said, 'are in a bad way.
They say that around the hotels the shoeshine boys are starv-
ing.' His face was triangular, pock-marked, saturnine. A heavy,
weary courtesy slowed his speech.

'What did you buy?' the second woman asked. She was
sallower than the other, and softer. Her English was the most
British-accented.

Clem showed them. 'Ah,' the man said, 'a scarab.'

'The incarnation of Khepri,' the green-eyed woman said.
'The symbol of immortality. You will live forever.' She smiled
at everything she said; he remembered her smiling with the
word 'remonstrate.'

'They're jolly things,' the other woman pronounced, in
her stately way. 'Dung beetles. They roll a ball of dung along
ahead of them, which appealed to the ancient Egyptians.
Reminded them of themselves, I suppose.'

'Life is that,' the man said. 'A ball of dung we push along.'

The waiter came and Clem said, 'Another whiskey sour.
And another round of whatever they're having.' Beer for
the man, Scotch for the taller lady, lemonade for his first
friend.

Having bought, he felt, the right to some education, Clem
asked, 'Seriously. Has the' – he couldn't bring himself to call
it a war, and he had noticed that in Egypt the words 'Israel'
and 'Israeli' were never pronounced – 'trouble cut down on
tourism?'

'Oh, immensely,' the taller lady said. 'Before the war, one
had to book for this boat months ahead. Now my husband
was granted two weeks and we were able to come at the last
moment. It is pathetic.'

'What do you do?' Clem asked.

The man made a self-deprecatory and evasive gesture, as
a deity might have, asked for employment papers.

'My brother,' the green-eyed woman stated, smiling, 'works for the government. In, what do you call it, planning?'

As if in apology for having been reticent, her brother abruptly said, 'The shoeshine boys and the dragomen suffer for us all. In everyone in my country, you have now a deep distress of humiliation.'

'I noticed,' Clem said, very carefully, 'those holes in the bridge we passed under.'

'They brought *Jeeps* in, Jeeps. By helicopter. The papers said bombs from a plane, but it was Jeeps by helicopters from the Red Sea. They drove onto the bridge, set the charges, and drove away. We are not warriors. We are farmers. For thousands of years now, we have had others do our fighting for us – Sudanese, Libyans, Arabs. We are not Arabs. We are Egyptians. The Syrians and Jordanians, they are Arabs – crazy men. But we, we don't know who we are, except we are very old. The man who seeks to make warriors of us creates distress.'

His wife put her hand on his to silence him while the waiter brought the drinks. His sister said to Clem, 'Are you enjoying our temples?'

'Quite.' But the temples within him, giant slices of limestone and sun, lay mute. 'I also quite like,' he went on, 'our guide. I admire the way he says everything in English to some of us and then in French to the rest.'

'Most Egyptians are trilingual,' the wife stated. 'Arabic, English, French.'

'Which do you think in?' Clem was concerned, for he was conscious in himself of an absence of verbal thoughts; instead, there were merely glints and reflections.

The sister smiled. 'In English, the thoughts are clearest. French is better for passion.'

'And Arabic?'

'Also for passion. Is it not so, Amina?'

'What so, Leila?' She had been murmuring with her husband.

The question was restated in French.

'Oh, *c'est vrai, vrai.*'

'How strange,' Clem said. 'English doesn't seem precise to me; quite the contrary. It's a mess of synonyms and lazy grammar.'

'No,' the wife said firmly – she never, he suddenly noticed, smiled – 'English is clear and cold, but not *nuancé* in the emotions, as is French.'

'And is Arabic *nuancé* in the same way?'

The green-eyed sister considered. 'More *angoisse.*'

Her brother said, 'We have ninety-nine words for "camel dung." All different states of camel dung. Camel dung, we understand.'

'Of course,' Leila said to Clem, 'Arabic here is nothing compared with the pure Arabic you would hear among the Saudis. The language of the Koran is so much more – can I say it? – gutsy. So guttural, nasal: strange, wonderful sounds. Amina, does it still affect you inwardly, to hear it chanted? The Koran.'

Amina solemnly agreed, 'It is terrible. It tears me all apart. It is too much passion.'

Italian rock music had entered the bar via an unseen radio, and one of the middle-aged English couples was trying to waltz to it. Noticing how intently Clem watched, the sister asked him, 'Do you like to dance?'

He took it as an invitation; he blushed. 'No, thanks, the fact is I can't.'

'Can't dance? Not at all?'

'I've never been able to learn. My mother says I have Methodist feet.'

'Your mother says that?' She laughed: a short shocking noise, the bark of a fox. She called to Amina, '*Sa mère dit que l'américain a les pieds méthodistes!*'

'*Les pieds méthodiques?*'

'*Non, non, aucune méthode, la secte chrétienne – méthodisme!*'

Both barked, and the man grunted. Clem sat there rigidly, immaculate in his embarrassment. Leila's green eyes, curious, pressed on him like gems scratching glass. The three Egyptians became overanimated, beginning sentences in one language and ending in another, and Clem understood that he was being laughed at. Yet the sensation, like the blurred plucking of the scarab salesmen, was better than untouched emptiness. He had another drink before dinner, the drink that was one too many, and when he went in to his single table, everything – the tablecloths, the little red lamps, the waiting droves of waiters in blue, the black windows beyond which the Nile glided – looked triumphant and glazed.

He slept badly. There were bumps and scraping above him, footsteps in the hall, the rumble of the motors, and, at four o'clock, the sounds of docking at another temple site. Once, he had found peace in hotel rooms, strange virgin corners where his mind could curl into itself, cut off from all nagging familiarities, and painlessly wink out. But he had known too many hotel rooms, so they had become themselves familiar, with their excessively crisp sheets and gleaming plumbing and easy chairs one never sat in but used as clothes racks. Only the pillows varied – neck-cracking fat bolsters in Leningrad, in Amsterdam hard little wads the size of a lady's purse, and as lumpy. Here on the floating hotel *Osiris*, two bulky pillows were provided and, toward morning, Clem discovered it relaxed him to put his head on one and his arms around the other. Some other weight in the bed seemed to be the balance that his agitated body, oscillating with hieroglyphs and sharp remonstrative glances, was craving. In his dream, the Egyptian women promised him something marvellous and showed him two tall limestone columns with blue sky between them. He awoke unrefreshed but conscious of having dreamed. On his ceiling there was a dance of light puzzling in its telegraphic rapidity, more like electronic art than anything natural. He analyzed it as sunlight bouncing off the tremulous Nile through the slats of his venetian blinds. He pulled the blinds and there it was again, stunning in its clarity: the blue river, the green strip, the pink cliffs, the unflecked sky. Only the village had changed. The other tourists – the Frenchman being slowly steered, like a fragile cart, by an Arab boy – were already heading up a flight of wooden stairs toward a bus. Clem ran after them, into the broad day, without shaving.

Their guide, Poppa Omar, sat them down in the sun in a temple courtyard and told them the story of Queen Hatshepsut. 'Remember it like this,' he said, touching his head and rubbing his chest. 'Hat – cheap – suit. She was wonderful woman here. Always building the temples, always winning the war and getting the nigger to be slaves. She marry her brother Tuthmosis and he grow tired here of jealous and insultation. He say to her, "O.K., you done a lot for Egypt, take it more easy now." She say to him, "No, I think I just keep rolling along." What happen? Tuthmosis die. The new king also Tuthmosis, her niece. He is a little boy. Hatshepsut show herself in all big statues wearing false beard and all flatness here.' He rubbed his chest. 'Tuthmosis get bigger and go say to her now, "Too much jealous and insultation. Take it easy for Egypt now." She say, "No." Then she die, and all over Egypt here, he take all her statue and smash, hit, hit, so

34

ot one face of Hatshepsut left and everywhere her name in
ll the walls here become Tuthmosis!' Clem looked around,
nd the statues had, indeed, been mutilated, thousands of
ears ago. He touched his own face and the whiskers
cratched.

On the way back in the bus, the Green Bay travelogue-
maker asked them to stop so he could photograph a water
vheel with his movie camera. A tiny child met them, weep-
ng, on the path, holding one arm as if crippled. '*Baksheesh,
aksheesh*,' he said. '*Musha, musha*.' One of the British men
licked at him with a whisk. The bald American announced
loud that the child was faking. Clem reached into his pocket
or a piaster coin, but then remembered himself as torturer.
eeing his gesture, the child, and six others, chased after him.
irst they shouted, then they tossed pebbles at his heels. From
vithin the haven of the bus, the tourists could all see the
hild's arm unbend. But the weeping continued and was
vidently real. The travelogist was still doing the water wheel,
nd the peddlers began to pry open the windows and thrust
n scarabs, dolls, alabaster vases not without beauty. The
vindow beside Clem's face slid back and a brown hand insin-
uated an irregular parcel about six inches long, wrapped in
rown cloth. 'Feesh mummy,' a disembodied voice said, and
o Clem it seemed hysterically funny. He couldn't stop laugh-
ng; the tip of his tongue began to hurt from being bitten.
The Scandinavian girl, across the aisle, glanced at him hope-
ully. Perhaps the crack in his surface was appearing.

Back on the *Osiris*, they basked in deck chairs. The white
oat had detached itself from the brown land, and men in
lue brought them lemonade, daiquiris, salty peanuts called
oudani. Though Clem, luminous with suntan oil, appeared
o be asleep, his lips moved in answer to Ingrid beside him.
Her bikini was chartreuse today. 'In my country,' she said,

'the summers are so short, naturally we take off our clothes. But it is absurd, this myth other countries have of our paganism, our happy sex. We are a harsh people. My father, he was like a man in the Bergman films. I was forbidden everything growing up – to play cards, lipstick, to dance.'

'I never did learn to dance,' Clem said, slightly shifting.

'Yes,' she said, 'I saw in you, too, a stern childhood. In place of harsh winters.'

'We had two yards of snow the other year,' Clem told her. 'In one storm. Two *meters*.'

'And yet,' Ingrid said, 'I think the thaw, when at last it comes in such places, is so dramatic, so intense.' She glanced toward him hopefully.

Clem appeared oblivious within his gleaming placenta of suntan oil.

The German boy who spoke a little English was on the other side of him. By now, the third day, the sunbathers had declared themselves: Clem, Ingrid, the two young Germans, the bald-headed American, the young English wife, whose skirted bathing suits were less immodest than her ordinary dresses. The rest of the British sat on the deck in the shade of the canopy and drank; the three Egyptians sat in the lounge and talked; the supposed Russians kept out of sight altogether. The travelogist was talking to the purser about the immense chain of tickets and reservations that would get him to Cape Town; the widow was in her cabin with Egyptian stomach and a burning passion to play bridge; the French couple sat by the rail, in the sun but fully dressed, reading guidebooks, his chair tipped back precariously, so he could see the gliding landscape.

The German boy asked Clem, 'Haff you bot a caftan?'

He had been nearly asleep, beneath a light, transparent headache. He said, '*Bitte?*'

'*Ein* caftan. You shoot. In Luxor; vee go back tonight. He ill measure you and haff it by morning, ven vee go. Sey are ood – wery cheap.'

Hatcheapsuit, Clem thought, but grunted that he might do . His frozen poise contended within him with a promiscuous nd American quality that must go forth and test, and purchase. le felt, having spurned so many scarabs and alabaster vases, hat he owed Egypt some of the large-leafed money that attened his wallet uncomfortably.

'It vood be wery handsome on you.'

'Ravishing,' the young English wife said behind them. She ad been listening. Clem sometimes felt like a mirror that veryone glanced into before moving on.

'You're all kidding me,' he announced. 'But I confess, I'm sucker for costumes.'

'Again,' Ingrid said, 'like a Bergman film.' And languorously he shifted her long arms and legs; the impression of flesh in he side of his vision disturbingly merged, in his sleepless tate, with a floating sensation of hollowness, of being in arentheses.

That afternoon they toured the necropolis in the Valley of he Kings. King Tut's small two-chambered tomb – how had hey crammed so much treasure in? The immense tunnels of Ramses III; or was it Ramses IV? Passageways hollowed from he limestone chip by chip, lit by systems of tilted mirrors, ainted with festive stiff figures banqueting, fishing, carrying fferings of fruit forward, which was always slightly down, lown past pits dug to entrap grave-robbers, past vast false hambers, toward the real and final one, a square room that vould have made a nice nightclub. Its murals had been left nfinished, sketched in gray ink but uncolored. The tremors f the artist's hand, his nervous strokes, were still there, over hree millennia later.

Abdul, the Egyptian planner, murmured to him, 'Always they left something unfinished; it is a part of their religion that no one understands. It is thought perhaps they dreaded finishing, as closing in the dead, limiting the life beyond.' They climbed up the long slanting passageway, threaded with electric lights, past hundreds of immaculate bodies carried without swing. 'The dead, you see, are not dead. In their language, the word for "death" and the word for "life" are the same. The death they feared was the second one, the one that would come if the tomb lacked provisions for life. In the tombs of the nobles, more than here, the scenes of life are all about, like a musical – you say "score"? – that only the dead have the instrument to play. These hieroglyphs are all instructions to the dead man, how to behave, how to make the safe journey.'

'Good planning,' Clem said, short of breath.

Abdul was slow to see the joke, since it was on himself.

'I mean the dead are much better planned for than the living.'

'No,' Abdul said flatly, perhaps misunderstanding. 'It is the same.'

Back in Luxor, Clem left the safe boat and walked toward the clothing shop, following the German boy's directions. He seemed to walk a long way. The narrowing streets grew shadowy. Pedestrians drifted by him in a steady procession, carrying offerings forward. No peddlers approached him; perhaps they all kept businessmen's hours, went home and totalled up the sold scarabs and fish mummies in double-entry ledgers. Radio Cairo blared and twanged from wooden balconies. Dusty intersections flooded with propaganda (or was it prayer?) faded behind him. The air was dark by the time he reached the shop. Within its little cavern of brightness, a young woman was helping a small child with homework, and a young man, the husband

and father, lounged against some stacked bolts of cloth. All three persons were petite; Egyptian children, Clem had observed before, are proportioned like miniature adults, with somber staring dolls' heads. He felt oversized in this shop, whose reduced scale was here and there betrayed by a coarse object from the real world – a steam press, a color print of Nasser on the wall. Clem's voice, asking if they could make a caftan for him by morning, seemed to boom; when he tuned it down, it cracked and trembled. Measuring him, the small man touched him all over; and touches that at first had been excused as accidental declared themselves as purposeful, determined.

'Hey,' Clem said, blushing.

Shielded from his wife by the rectangular bulk of Clem's body, the young man, undoing his own fly with a swift light tailor's gesture, exhibited himself. 'I can make you very happy,' he muttered.

'I'm leaving,' Clem said.

He was at the doorway instantly, but the tailor had time to call, 'Sir, when will you come back tomorrow?' Clem turned; the little man was zipped, the woman and child had their heads bent together over the homework. Nasser, a lurid ochre, scowled toward the future. Clem had intended to abandon the caftan but pictured himself back in Buffalo, wearing it to New Year's Eve at the country club, with sunglasses and sandals. The tailor looked frightened. His little mustache twitched uncertainly and his brown eyes had been worn soft by needlework.

Clem said he would be back no later than nine. The boat sailed south after breakfast. Outside, the dry air had chilled. From the tingling at the tip of his tongue, he realized he had been smiling hard.

Ingrid was sitting at the bar in a backwards silver dress, high in the front and buckled at the back. She invited herself to

39

John Updike

sit at his table during dinner; her white arms, pinched pink by the sun, shared in the triumphant glaze of the tablecloth, the glowing red lamp. They discussed religion. Clem had been raised as a Methodist, she as a Lutheran. In her father's house, north of Stockholm, there had been a guest room held ready against the arrival of Jesus Christ. Not quite seriously, it had been a custom, and yet . . . She supposed religion had bred into her a certain *expectancy*. Into him, he responded, groping, peering with difficulty into that glittering blank area which in other people, he imagined, was the warm cave of self – into him the Methodist religion had bred a certain compulsive neatness, a *dislike of litter*. It was a disappointing answer, even after he had explained the word 'litter.' Reckless on his third pre-dinner drink, he advanced the theory that he was a royal tomb, once crammed with treasure, that had been robbed. Her white hand moved an inch toward him on the tablecloth, intelligent as a bat, and he began to cry. The tears felt genuine to him, but she said, 'Stop acting.'

He told her that a distressing thing had just happened to him.

She said, 'That is your flaw; you are too self-conscious. You are always in costume, acting. You must always be beautiful.' She was so intent on delivering this sermon that only as an afterthought did she ask him what had been the distressing thing.

He found he couldn't tell her; it was too intimate, and his own part in provoking it had been, he felt, unspeakably shameful. The tailor's homosexual advance had been, like the child's feigning a crippled arm, evoked by his money, his torturing innocence. He said, 'Nothing. I've been sleeping badly and don't make sense. Ingrid: have some more wine.' His palms were sweating from the effort of pronouncing her name.

After dinner, though fatigue was making his entire body

40

shudder and itch, she asked him to take her into the lounge, where a three-piece band from Alexandria was playing dance music. The English couples waltzed. Gwenn, the young wife, frugged with one of the German boys. The green-eyed Egyptian woman danced with the purser. Egon, the German boy who knew some English, came and, with a curt bow and a curious hard stare at Clem, invited Ingrid. She danced, Clem observed, very close, in the manner of one who, puritanically raised, thinks of it only as a substitute for intercourse. After many numbers, she was returned to him unmarred, still silver, cool, and faintly admonitory. Downstairs, in the corridor where their cabin doors were a few steps apart, she asked him, her expression watchful and stern, if he would sleep better tonight. Compared with her large eyes and long nose, her mouth was small; she pursed her lips in a thoughtful pout, holding as if in readiness a small dark space between them.

He realized that her face was stern because he was a mirror in which she was gauging her beauty, her power. His smile sought to reassure her. 'Yes,' he said, 'I'm sure I will. I'm dead beat, frankly.'

And he did fall asleep quickly, but woke in the dark, to escape a dream in which the hieroglyphs and pharaonic cartouches had left the incised walls and inverted and become stamps, sharp-edged stamps trying to indent themselves upon him. Awake, he identified the dream blows with the thumping of feet and furniture overhead. He could not sink back into sleep; there was a scuttling, an occasional whispering in the corridor that he felt was coming toward him, toward his door. But once, when he opened his door, there was nothing in the corridor but bright light and several pairs of shoes. The problem of the morning prevented him from sinking back. If he went to pick up his caftan, it would seem to the tailor a submission. He would be misunderstood and vulnerable. Also, there was the danger of missing the boat. Yet the caftan would be lovely to have, a shimmering striped polished cotton, with a cartouche containing Clem's monogram in silver thread. In his agitation, his desire not to make a mistake, he could not achieve peace with his pillows; and then the telegraphic staccato of sunlight appeared on his ceiling and Egypt, that green thread through the desert, was taut and bright beyond his blinds. Leaving breakfast, light-headed, he impulsively approached the bald American on the stairs. 'I beg your pardon; this is rather silly, but could you do me an immense favor?'

'Like what?'

'Just walk with me up to this shop where something I ordered should be waiting. Uh . . . it's embarrassing to explain.'

'The boat's pulling out in half an hour.'

'I know.'

The man sized Clem up – his clean shirt, his square shoulders, his open hopeful face – and grunted, 'O.K. I left my whisk in the cabin, I'll see you outside.'

'Gee, I'm very grateful, uh –'

'Walt's the name.'

Ingrid, coming up the stairs late to breakfast, had overheard. 'May I come, too, on this expedition that is so dangerous?'

'No, it's stupid,' Clem told her. 'Please eat your breakfast. I'll see you on the deck afterward.'

Her face attempted last night's sternness, but she was puffy beneath her eyes from sleep, and he revised upward his estimate of her age. Like him, she was over thirty. How many men had she passed through to get here, alone; how many self-forgetful nights, traumatic mornings of separation,

42

hungover heartbroken afternoons? It was epic to imagine, her history of love; she loomed immense in his mind, a monumental statue, forbidding and foreign, even while under his nose she blinked and puckered her lips, rejected. She went into breakfast alone.

On the walk to the shop, Clem tried to explain what had happened the evening before. Walt impatiently interrupted. 'They're scum,' he said. 'They'll sell their mother for twenty piasters.' His accent still had Newark gravel in it. A boy ran shyly beside them, offering them *soudani* from a bowl. 'Amscray,' Walt said, brandishing his whisk.

'Is very good,' the boy said.

'You make me puke,' Walt told him.

The woman and the boy doing homework were gone from the shop. Unlit, it looked dingy; Nasser's glass was cracked. The tailor sprang up when they entered, pleased and relieved. 'I work all night,' he said.

'Like hell you did,' Walt said.

'Try on?' the tailor asked Clem.

In the flecked dim mirror, Clem saw himself gowned; a shock, because the effect was not incongruous. He looked like a husky woman, a bigboned square-faced woman, quick to blush and giggle, the kind of naïve healthy woman, with money and without many secrets, that he tended to be attracted to. He had once loved such a girl, and she had snubbed him to marry a Harvard man. 'It feels tight under the armpits,' he said.

The tailor rapidly caressed and patted his sides. 'That is its cut,' he said.

'And the cartouche was supposed to be in silver thread.'

'You said gold.'

'I said silver.'

'Don't take it,' Walt advised.

'I work all night,' the tailor said.

'And here,' Clem said. 'This isn't a pocket, it's just a slit.'

'No, no, no pocket. Supposed to let the hand through. Here, I show.' He put his hand in the slit and touched Clem until Clem protested, 'Hey.'

'I can make you very happy,' the tailor murmured.

'Throw it back in his face,' Walt said. 'Tell him it's a god-awful mess.'

'No,' Clem said. 'I'll take it. The fabric is lovely. If it turns out to be too tight, I can give it to my mother.' He was sweating so hard that the garment became stuck as he tried to pull it over his head, and the tailor, assisting him, was an enveloping blur of caresses.

From within the darkness of cloth, Clem heard a slap and Walt's voice snarl, 'Hands off, sonny.' The subdued tailor swiftly wrapped the caftan in brown paper. As Clem paid, Walt said, 'I wouldn't buy that rag. Throw it back in his face.' Outside, as they hurried back toward the boat, through crowded streets where women clad all in black stepped sharply aside, guarding their faces against the evil eye, Walt said, 'The little queer.'

'I don't think it meant anything, it was just a nervous habit. But it scared me. Thanks a lot for coming along.'

Walt asked him, 'Ever try it with a man?'

'No. Good heavens.'

Walt said, 'It's not bad.' He nudged Clem in walking and Clem shifted his parcel to that side, as a shield. All the way to the boat, Walt's conversation was anecdotal and obscene, describing a night he had had in Alexandria and another in Khartoum. Twice Clem had to halt and shift to Walt's other side, to keep from being nudged off the sidewalk. 'It's not bad,' Walt insisted. 'It'd pleasantly surprise you, I guarantee it. Don't have a closed mind.'

Back on the *Osiris*, Clem locked the cabin door while changing into his bathing suit. The engines shivered; the boat glided away from the Luxor quay. On deck, Ingrid asked him if his dangerous expedition had been successful. She had reverted to the orange bikini.

'I got the silly thing, yes. I don't know if I'll ever wear it.'

'You must model it tonight; we are having Egyptian Night.'

Her intonation saying this was firm with reserve. Her air of pique cruelly pressed upon him in his sleepless, sensitive, brittle state. Ingrid's lower lip jutted in profile; her pale eyes bulged beneath the spears of her lashes. He tried to placate her by describing the tailor shop – its enchanted smallness, the woman and child bent over schoolwork.

'It is a farce,' Ingrid said, with a bruising positiveness, 'their schooling. They teach the poor children the language of the Koran, which is difficult and useless. The literacy statistics are nonsense.'

Swirls of Arabic, dipping like bird flight from knot to knot, wound through Clem's brain and gently tugged him downward into a softness where Ingrid's tan body stretching beside him merged with the tawny strip of desert gliding beyond the ship's railing. Lemonade was being served to kings around him. On the ceiling of a temple chamber that he had seen, the goddess Nut was swallowing the sun in one corner and giving birth to it in another, all out of the same body. A body was above him and words were crashing into him like stones. He opened his eyes; it was the American widow, a broad cloud of cloth eclipsing the sun, a perfumed mass of sweet-voiced anxiety resurrected from her cabin, crying out to him, 'Young man, you *look* like a bridge player. We're *des*perate for a fourth!'

The caftan pinched him under the arms; and then, later in Egyptian Night, after the meal, Ingrid danced with Egon and

45

disappeared. To these discomforts the American widow and Walt added that of their company. Though Clem had declined her bridge invitation, his protective film had been broken and they had plunked themselves down around the little table where Clem and Ingrid were eating the buffet of *foule* and pilaf and *qualeema* and falafel and *maamoule*. To Clem's surprise, the food was to his taste – nutty, bland, dry. Then Ingrid was invited to dance and failed to return to the table, and the English couples, who had befriended the widow, descended in a cloud of conversation.

'This place was a hell of a lot more fun under Farouk,' said the old man with a scoured red face.

'At least the poor *fellah*,' a woman perhaps his wife agreed, 'had a little glamour and excitement to look up to.'

'Now what does the poor devil have? A war he can't fight and Soviet slogans.'

'They *hate* the Russians, of course. The average Egyptian, he loves a show of style, and the Russians don't have any. Not a crumb.'

'The poor dears.'

And they passed on to ponder the inability, mysterious but proven a thousand times over, of Asiatics and Africans – excepting, of course, the Israelis and the Japanese – to govern themselves or, for that matter, to conduct the simplest business operation efficiently. Clem was too tired to talk and too preoccupied with the pressure chafing his armpits, but they all glanced into his face and found their opinions reflected there. In a sense, they deferred to him, for he was prosperous and young and as an American the inheritor of their colonial wisdom.

All had made attempts at native costume. Walt wore his pajamas, and the widow, in bedsheet and sunglasses and *kaffiyeh*, did suggest a fat sheik, and Gwenn's husband had blacked his face with an ingenious paste of Bain de Soleil and instant coffee. Gwenn asked Clem to dance. Blushing, he declined, but she insisted. 'There's nothing to it – you simply bash yourself about a bit,' she said, and demonstrated.

She was dressed as a harem girl. For her top, she had torn the sleeves off one of her husband's shirts and left it unbuttoned, so that a strip of skin from the base of her throat to her navel was bare; she was not wearing a bra. Her pantaloons were less successful: yellow St.-Tropez slacks pinned in loosely below the knees. A blue gauze scarf across her nose – setting her hectic English cheeks and heavily lashed Twiggy eyes eerily afloat – and gold chains around her ankles completed the costume. The band played 'Delilah.' As Clem watched Gwenn's bare feet, their shuffle, and the glitter of gold, and the ten silver toenails seemed to be rapidly writing something indecipherable. There was a quick half-step she seemed unaware of, in counterpoint with her swaying head and snaking arms. 'Why – oh – whyyy, De-liii-lah,' the young Egyptian sang in a Liverpool whine. Clem braced his body, hoping the pumping music would possess it. His feet felt sculpturally one with the floor; it was like what stuttering must be for the tongue. The sweat of incapacity fanned outward from the pain under his arms, but Gwenn obliviously rolled on, her pantaloons coming unpinned, her shirt loosening so that, as she swung from side to side, one shadowy breast, and now the other, was entirely revealed. She had shut her eyes, and in the shelter of her blindness Clem did manage to dance a little, to shift his weight and jerk his arms, though he was able to do it only by forgetting the music. The band changed songs and rhythms without his noticing; he was conscious mostly of the skirt of his caftan swinging around him, of Gwenn's English cheeks burning and turning below sealed slashes of mascara, and of her husband's stained face. He had come onto the dance floor with the American widow; as the Bain de Soleil had sunk into his skin, the instant coffee had powdered his galabia. At last the band took a break. Gwenn's husband claimed her, and Leila, the green-eyed Egyptian woman, as Clem passed her table, said remonstratingly, 'You *can* dance.'

'He is a dervish,' Amina stated.

'All Americans are dervishes,' Abdul sighed. 'Their energy menaces the world.'

'I am the world's worst dancer; I'm hopeless,' Clem said.

'Then you should sit,' Leila said. All three Egyptians were dressed, disdainfully, in Western dress. Clem ordered a renewal of their drinks and a brandy for himself.

'Tell me,' he begged Abdul. 'Do you think the Russians have no style?'

'It is true,' Abdul said. 'They are a very ugly people. Their clothes are very baggy. They are like us, Asiatic. They are not yet convinced that this world absolutely matters.'

'*Mon mari veut créer une grande théorie politique,*' Amina said to Clem.

Clem persisted. Fatigue made him desperate and dogged. 'But,' he said, 'I was surprised, in Cairo, even now, with our ambassador kicked out, and all these demonstrations, how many Americans were standing around the lobby of the Hilton. And all the American movies.'

'For a time,' Amina said, 'they tried films only from the Soviet Union and China, about farming progressively. The theater managers handed their keys in to the government and said, "Here, you run them." No one would come. So the Westerns came back.'

'And this music,' Clem said, 'and your clothes.'

'Oh, we love you,' Abdul said, 'but with our brains. You

are like the stars, like the language of the Koran. We know we cannot be like that. There is a sullen place' – he moved his hand from his head to his stomach – 'where the Russians make themselves at home.'

The waiter brought the drinks and Amina said 'Shh' to her husband.

Leila said to Clem, 'You have changed girlfriends tonight. You have many girlfriends.'

He blushed. 'None.'

Leila said, 'The big Swede, she danced very close with the German boy. Now they have both gone off.'

'Into the Nile?' Amina asked. 'Into the desert? How jolly romantic.'

Abdul said slowly, as if bestowing comfort, 'They are both Nordic. They are at home within each other. Like us and the Russians.'

Leila seemed angry. Her green eyes flashed and Clem feared they would seek to scratch his face. Instead, her ankle touched Clem's beneath the table; he flinched. 'They are both,' she said, 'ice – ize –? They hang down in winter.'

'Icicles?' Clem offered.

She curtly nodded, annoyed at needing rescue. 'I have never seen one,' she said in self-defense.

'Your friends the British,' Abdul said, indicating the noisy table where they were finger-painting on Gwenn's husband's face, 'understood us in their fashion. They had read Shakespeare. It is very good, that play. How we turned our sails and ran. Our cleverness and courage are all female.'

'I'm sure that's not so,' Clem protested.

Leila snapped, 'Why should it not be so? All countries are women, except horrid Uncle Sam.' And though he sat at their table another hour, her ankle did not touch his again.

Floating on three brandies, Clem at last left the lounge,

his robe of polished cotton swinging around him. The Frenchman was tipped back precariously in a corner, watching the dancers. He lifted his mirror in salute as Clem passed. Though even the Frenchman's wife was dancing, Ingrid had not returned, and this added to Clem's lightness, his freedom from litter. Surely he would sleep. But when he lay down on his bed, it was trembling and jerking. His cabin adjoined that of the unsociable plump couple thought to be Russian. Clem's bed and one of theirs were separated by a thin partition. His shuddered as theirs heaved with a playful, erratic violence; there was a bump, a giggle, a hoarse male sibilance. Then the agitation settled toward silence and a distinct rhythm, a steady, mounting beat that put a pulsing into the bed taut under Clem. Two or three minutes of this. Then: 'Oh.' The woman's exclamation was at a middle pitch, gender-neutral; a man's guttural grunt came right on top of it. Clem's bed, in its abrupt stillness, seemed to float and spin under him. Then, from beyond the partition, some murmurs, a sprinkling of laughter, the word '*Khorosho*,' and a resonant heave as one body left the bed. Soon, twin snoring. Clem had been robbed of the gift of sleep.

After shapeless hours of pillow wrestling, he went to the window and viewed the Nile gliding by, the constellations of village lights, and the desert stars, icy in their clarity. He wanted to open the window to smell the river and the desert, but it was sealed shut, in deference to the air conditioning. Clem remembered Ingrid and a cold silver rage, dense as an ingot, upright as an obelisk, filled his body. 'You bitch,' he said aloud and, by repeating those two words, over and over, leaving his mind no space to entertain any other images, he managed to wedge himself into a few hours' sleep, despite the tempting, problematical scuttle of presences in the hall, who now and then brushed his door with their fingernails.

You bitch, you bitch, you . . . He remembered nothing about his dreams, except that they all took place back in Buffalo, amid aunts and uncles he had thought he had forgotten.

Temples. Dour, dirty, heavy Isna sunk in its great pit beside a city market where Clem, pestered by flies and peddlers, nearly vomited at the sight of ox palates, complete with arcs of teeth, hung up for sale. Vast sunstruck Idfu, an endless square spiral climb up steps worn into troughs toward a dizzying view, the amateur travelogist calmly grinding away on the unparapeted edge. Cheery little Kom Ombo, right by the Nile, whiter and later than the others. In one of them, dead Osiris was resurrected by a hawk alighting on his phallus; in another, Nut the sky goddess flowed above them nude, swimming amid gilt stars. A god was having a baby, baby Horus. Poppa Omar bent over and tenderly patted the limestone relief pitted and defaced by Coptic Christians. 'See now here,' he said, 'the lady squat, and the other ladies hold her by the arms so, here, and the baby Horus, out he comes here. In villages all over Egypt now, the ladies there still have the babies in such manner, so we have too many the babies here.' He looked up at them and smiled with unflecked benevolence. His eyes, surprisingly, were pale blue.

The travelogist from Wisconsin was grinding away, Walt from New Jersey was switching his whisk, the widow was fainting in the shade, beside a sphinx. Clem helped the Frenchman inch his feet across some age-worn steps; he was like one of those toys that walk down an inclined ramp but easily topple. The English and Egyptians were bored: too many temples, too much Ramses. Ingrid detached herself from the German boys and came to Clem. 'How did you sleep?'

'Horribly. And you?'

'Well. Very well. I thought,' she added, 'you would be soothed by my no longer trying to rape you.'

At noon, in the sun, as the *Osiris* glided toward Aswan, she took her accustomed chair beside Clem. When Egon left the chair on the other side of him and clamorously swam in the pool, Clem asked her, 'How is he?'

'He is very nice,' she said, holding her bronze face immobile in the sun. 'Very earnest, very naïve. He is a revolutionary.'

'I'm glad,' he said, 'you've found someone congenial.'

'Have I? He is very young. Perhaps I went with him to make another jealous.' She added, expressionless, 'Did it?'

'Yes.'

'I am pleased to hear it.'

In the evening, she was at the bar when he went up from an unsuccessful attempt at a nap. They had docked for the last time; the boat had ceased trembling. She had reverted to the silver dress that looked put on backwards. He asked, 'Where are the Germans?'

'They are with the Egyptians in the lounge. Shall we join them?'

'No,' Clem said. Instead, they talked with the lanky man from Green Bay, who had ten months of advance tickets and reservations to Cape Town and back, including a homeward cabin on the *Queen Elizabeth II*. He spoke mostly to women's groups and high schools, and he detested the Packers. He said to Clem, 'I take pride in being an eccentric, don't you?' and Clem was frightened to think that he appeared eccentric, he who had always been praised, even teased, by his mother as typically American, as even *too* normal and dependable. She sometimes implied that he had disappointed her by not defying her, by always dutifully returning from his trips alone.

After dinner, he and Ingrid walked in Aswan: a receding quay of benches, open shops burning a single lightbulb, a swish of vehicles, mostly military. A true city, where the appetites are served. He had bought some postcards and let a boy shine his dusty shoes. He paid the boy ten piasters, shielding his potent wallet with his body. They returned to the *Osiris* and sat in the lounge watching the others dance. A chaste circle around them forbade intrusion; or perhaps the others, having tried to enter Clem and failed, had turned away. Clem imagined them in the eyes of the others, both so composed and now so tan, two stately cool children of harsh winters. Apologizing, smiling, after three iced attacks, he bit his tongue and rose. 'Forgive me, I'm dead. I must hit the hay. You stay and dance.'

She shook her head, with a preoccupied stern gesture, gathered her dress tight about her hips, and went with him. In the hall before his door, she stood and asked, 'Don't you want me?'

A sudden numbness lifted from his stomach and made him feel giddily tall. 'Yes,' he said.

'Then why not take me?'

Clem looked within himself for the answer, saw only glints refracted and distorted by a deep fatigue. 'I'm frightened to,' he told her. 'I have no faith in my right to take things.'

Ingrid listened intently, as if his words were continuing, clarifying themselves; she looked at his face and nodded. Now that they had come so far together and were here, her gaze seemed soft, as soft and weary as the tailor's. 'Go to your room,' she said. 'If you like, then, I will come to you.'

'Please do.' It was as simple, then, as dancing – you simply bash yourself about a bit.

'Would you like me to?' She was stern now, could afford to be guarded.

'Yes. *Please* do.'

He left the latch off, undressed, washed, brushed his teeth, shaved the second time that day, left the bathroom light on. The bed seemed immensely clean and taut, like a sail. Strange stripes, nonsense patterns, crossed his mind. The sail held taut, permitting a gliding, but with a tipping. The light in the cabin changed. The door had been opened and shut. She was still wearing the silver dress; Clem had imagined she would change. She sat on his bed; her weight was the counterweight he had been missing. He curled tighter, as if around a pillow, and an irresistible peace descended, distinctly, from the four corners of space, along forty-five-degree angles marked in charcoal. He opened his eyes, discovering thereby that they had been shut, and the sight of her back – the belling solidity of her bottom, the buckle of the backwards belt, the scoop of cloth exposing the nape of blond neck and the strong crescent of shoulder waiting to be touched – covered his eyes with silver scales. On one of the temple walls, one of the earlier ones, Poppa Omar had read off the hieroglyphs that spelled *Woman is Paradise*. The moored ship and its fittings were still. Confident she would not move, he postponed the beginning for one more second.

He awoke feeling rich, full of sleep. At breakfast, he met Ingrid by the glass dining-room doors and apologetically smiled, blushing and biting his tongue. 'God, I'm sorry,' he said. He added in self-defense, 'I told you I was dead.'

'It was charming,' she said. 'You gave yourself to me that way.'

'How long did you sit there?'

'Perhaps an hour. I tried to insert myself into your dreams. Did you dream of me?' She was a shade shy, asking.

He remembered no dreams but did not say so. Her eyes were permanently soft now toward him; they had become windows through which he could admire himself. It did not occur to him that he might admire her in the same fashion: in the morning light, he saw clearly the traces of age on her face and throat, the little scars left by time and a presumed promiscuity, for which he, though not heavily, did blame her. His defect was that, though accustomed to reflect love, he could not originate light within himself; he was as blind as the silvered side of a mirror to the possibility that he, too, might impose a disproportionate glory upon the form of another. The world was his but slid through him.

In the morning, they went by felucca to Lord Kitchener's gardens, and the Aga Khan's tomb, where a single rose was fresh in a vase. The afternoon expedition, and their last, was to the Aswan High Dam. Cameras were forbidden. They saw the anti-aircraft batteries and the worried brown soldiers in their little wooden cartoon guardhouses. The desert became very ugly: no longer the rose shimmer that had surrounded him at the airport in Luxor, it was a merciless gray that had never entertained a hope of life, not even fine in texture but littered to the horizon with black flint. And the makeshift pitted roads were ugly, and the graceless Russian machinery clanking and sitting stalled, and the styleless, already squalid propaganda pavilion containing a model of the dam. The dam itself, after the straight, elegantly arched dam the British had built down-river, seemed a mere mountain of heaped rubble, hardly distinguishable from the inchoate desert itself. Yet at its heart, where the turbines had been set, a plume like a cloud of horses leaped upward in an inverted Niagara that dissolved, horse after horse, into mist before becoming the Nile again and flowing on. Startled greenery flourished on the gray cliffs that contained the giant plume. The stocky couple who had been impassive and furtive for six days beamed and crowed aloud; the man roughly nudged Clem to wake him to the wonder of what they were seeing. Clem agreed '*Khorosho.*' He waited but was not nudged again. Gazing into the abyss of the trip that was over, he saw that he had been happy.

POCKET PENGUINS

POCKET PENGUINS